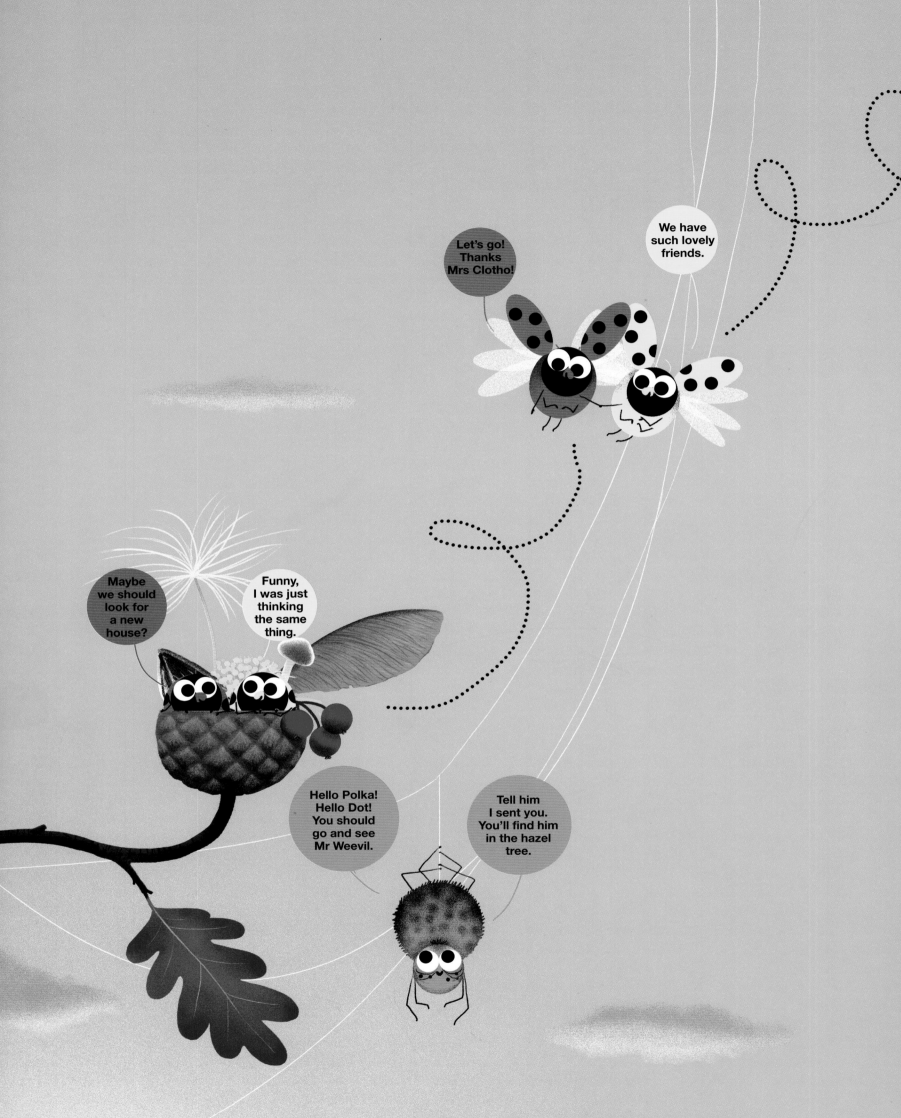

First published 2012 by order of the Tate Trustees by Tate Publishing, a division of Tate Enterprises Ltd, Millbank, London SW1P 4RG
www.tate.org.uk/publishing
First published in French as Coccinelles cherchent maison © 2011 Editions Sarbacane, Paris. This edition © Tate 2012.
All rights reserved.
A catalogue record for this book is available from the British Library
ISBN 978 1 84976 100 0
Distributed in the United States and Canada by ABRAMS, New York
Library of Congress Control Number: applied for
Printed in Malaysia

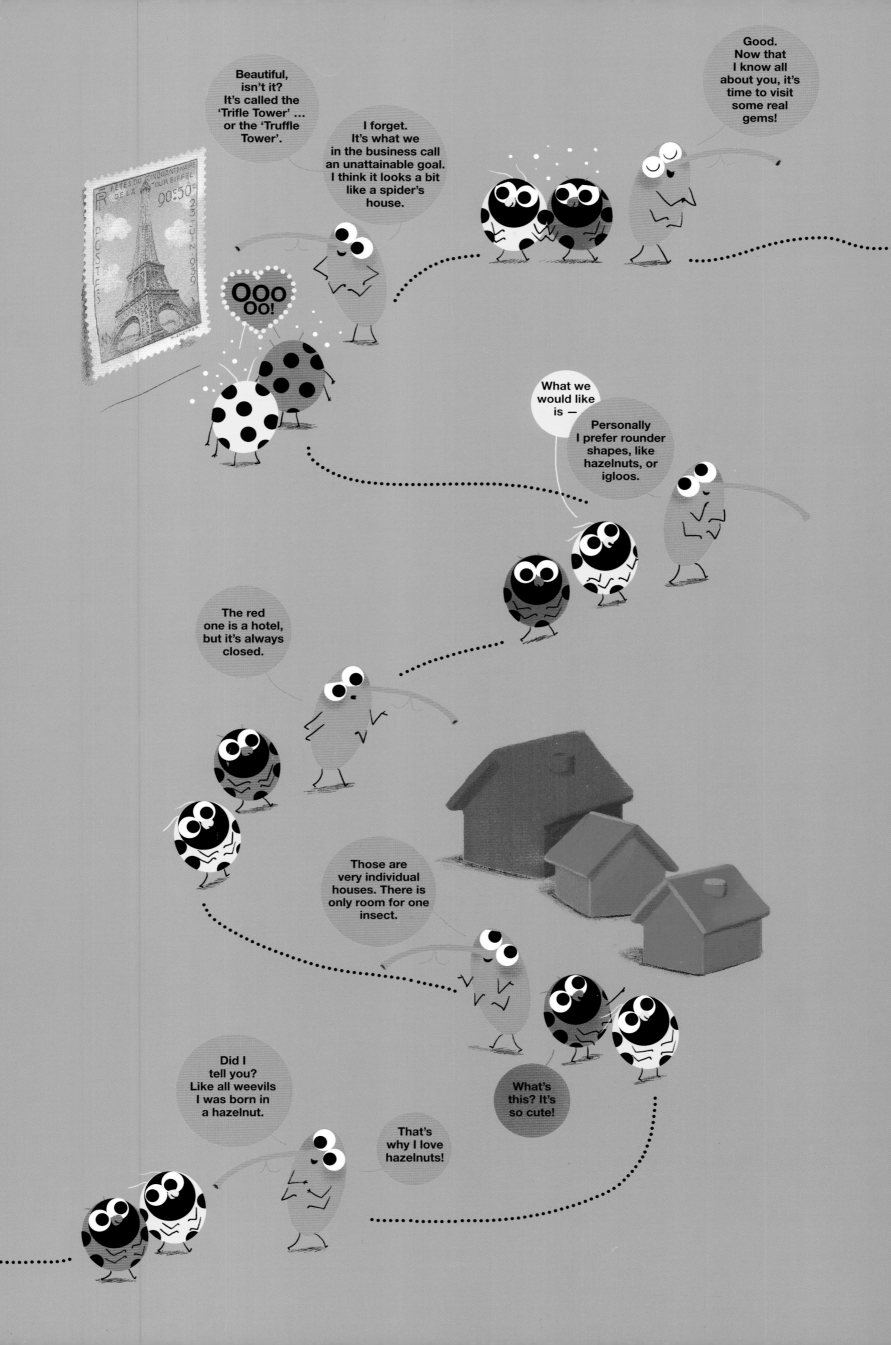

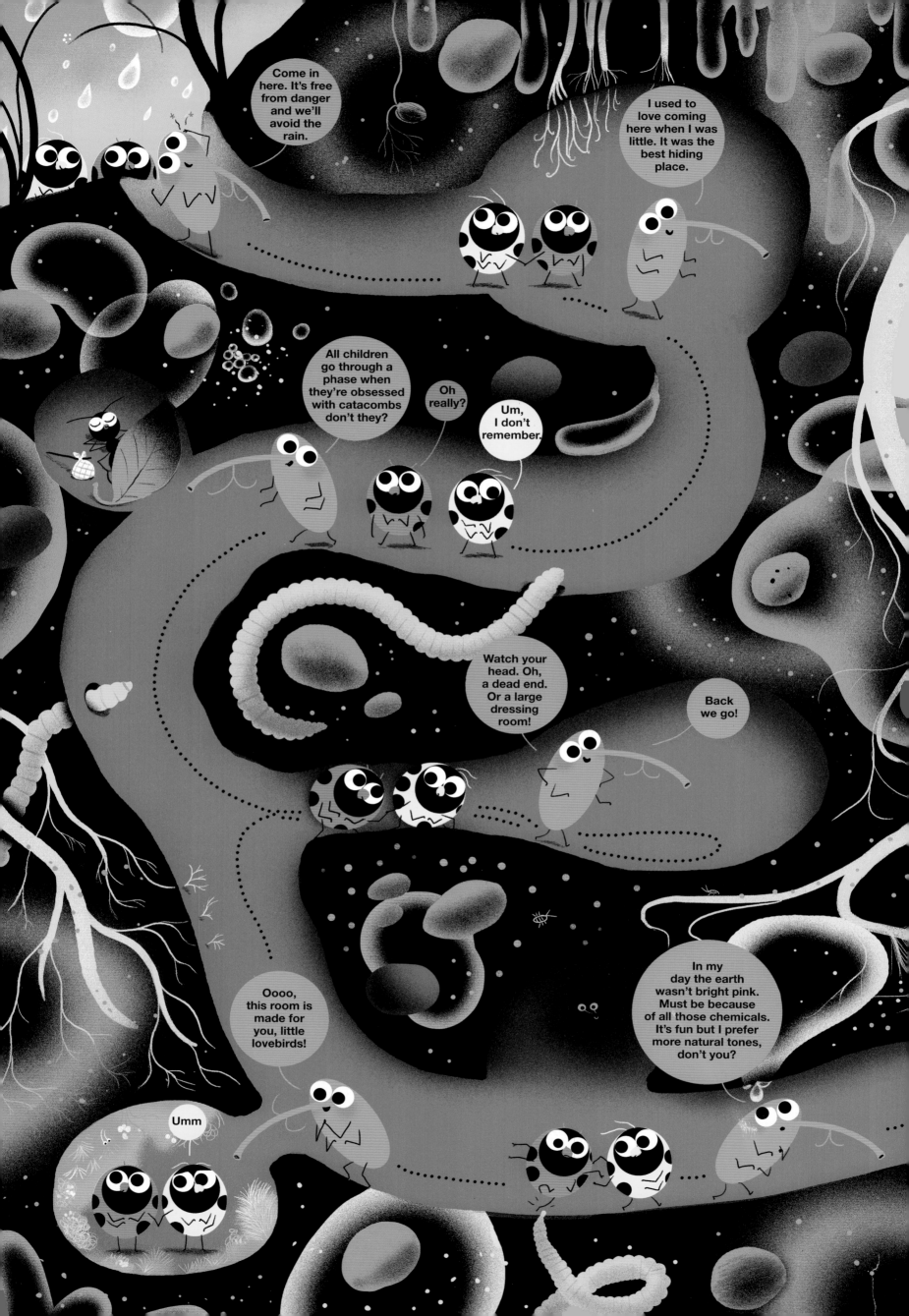

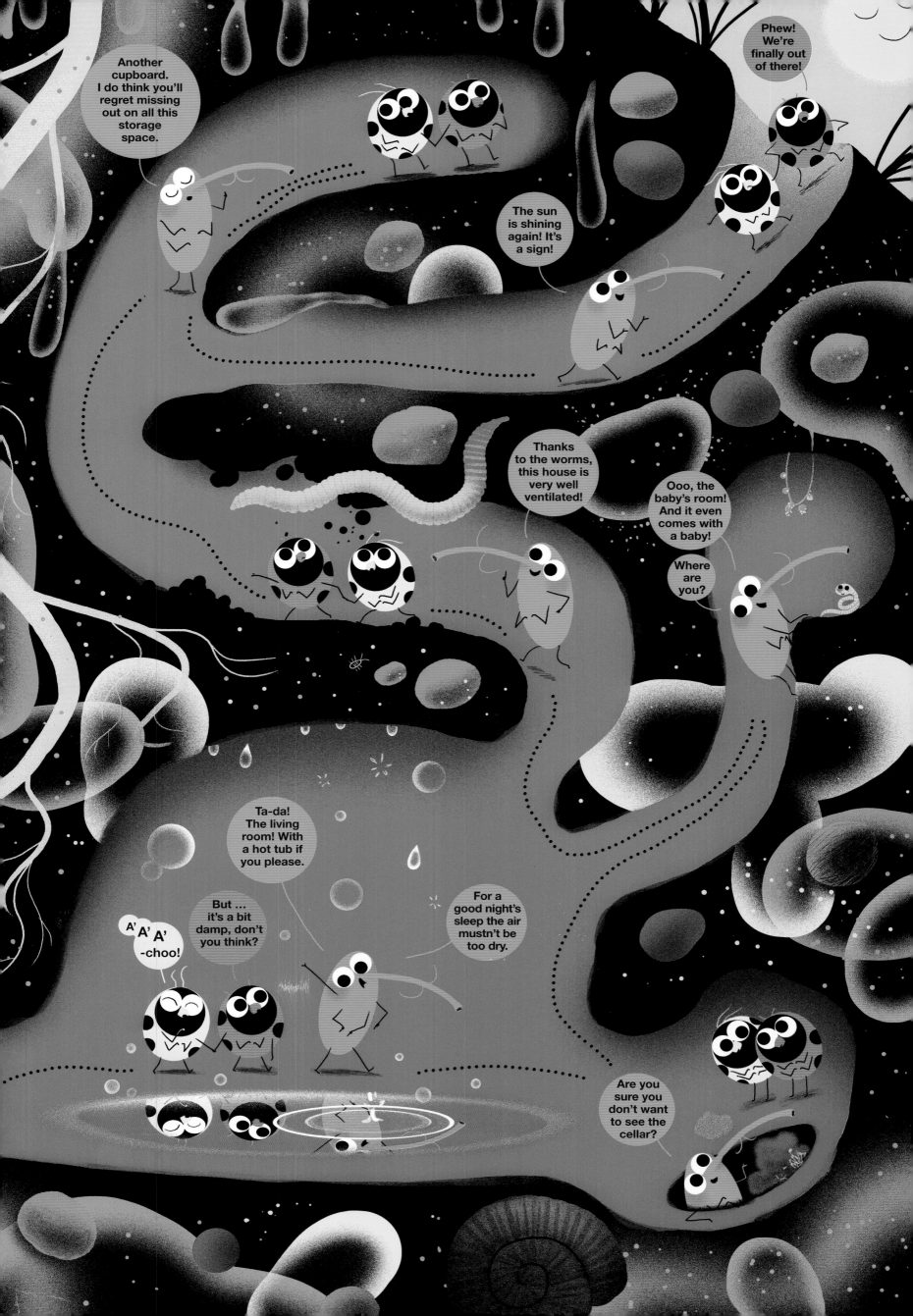

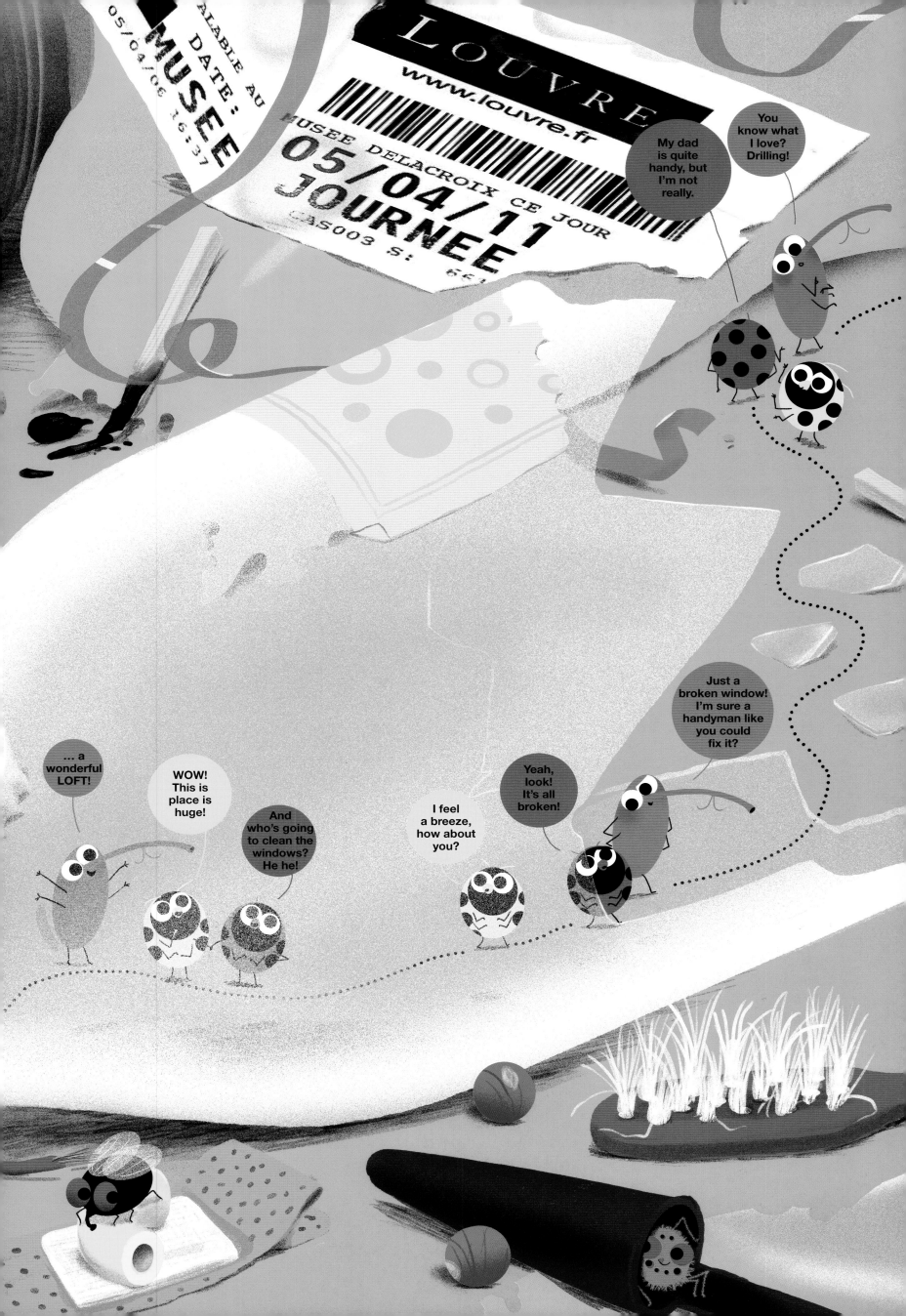